The Horse
That Liked
Sandwiches

The Horse

by Vivian L. Thompson
illustrated by Aliki

G. P. Putnam's Sons
New York

That Liked Sandwiches

To Odessa Davenport

© 1962 by Vivian L. Thompson and Aliki Brandenberg
Library of Congress càtalog card number: 62-8718
All rights reserved
MANUFACTURED IN THE UNITED STATES OF AMERICA
Published simultaneously in the Dominion of Canada
by Longmans, Green and Company, Toronto

Fifth Impression

MARIO

The Horse That Liked Sandwiches

MARIO was a big black work horse. He worked for Tony, pulling a wagon filled with fresh fruit. Up and down the streets they went, in the country, and in the town.

Mario was a good horse. He worked hard. He never made trouble, except when he was hunting for sandwiches. Mario liked sandwiches! He could never get enough of them. Chicken sandwiches, egg sandwiches, peanut butter and jam sandwiches. He liked them all.

Each day at lunch time, Tony had sandwiches. Mario had a bag of oats. Mario always wanted to trade lunches with Tony, but Tony didn't like oats very much.

It was Monday morning. Mario and Tony started out. Up and down the streets they went, and out into the country. At lunch time, they stopped. It was a warm day. Tony ate his lunch and took a nap. Mario ate his lunch and went for a walk.

In a big field, he saw a woman and
a little boy. They had a picnic lunch.
Sandwiches!
The little boy gave Mario one.
Chicken!
It was good. He ate it all.

Mario looked at the woman.

"Oh no!" said the woman. "You may not have my sandwich!"

Her sweater lay on the grass. She hid the sandwich inside. Mario went closer. The woman left her sandwich and ran. Mario found the sandwich.

Egg! It was good. He ate it all. The woman was cross. "I will see about this!" she said.

Tuesday came. Mario and Tony started out. Up and down the streets they went, and out into the country. At lunch time, they stopped. It was a hot day. Tony ate his lunch and took a nap. Mario ate his lunch and went for a walk. Down by the river, Mario saw a man fishing.

There was a basket near him.
Sandwiches?
Mario opened the basket.
No sandwiches!
Mario pushed the basket into the river. The fisherman was angry. "I am going to do something about this!" he said.

Wednesday came. Mario and Tony started out. Out into the country they went, on into the woods, and back into town. At lunch time, they stopped. It was a very hot day. Tony ate his lunch and took a nap. Mario ate his lunch and went for a walk.

Mario looked around. No trees, no river, no cool place to rest. Mario came back and lay down in the road. Along came a car. The driver sounded his horn. Mario opened his eyes and looked around.

No sandwiches!

He closed his eyes and went back to sleep. Tony could not make Mario move. The driver had to back up and go another way. He was very angry. "I will tell the Police Chief about this!" he said.

Thursday came. A policeman came to Tony's house. He said, "Tony, the Police Chief wants to see you. Bring Mario with you."

Down the street went the policeman. Down the street went Mario and Tony, all the way to the Town Hall.

The Police Chief stood outside.

"Here they are, Chief," said the policeman. "And here is your lunch. You forgot it this morning."

"Thank you," said the Police Chief. "Just put it down some place."

The Police Chief looked at Tony. He said, "I have been hearing things about Mario. This lady says he ripped her sweater. This man says Mario pushed his basket into the river. This man says Mario made him late for a meeting. What have you got to say?"

IMMACULATA COLLEGE
HAMBURG, NEW YORK

Tony said, "Mario is a good horse, Chief. He works hard. He never makes trouble except when he goes hunting for sandwiches."

"He made trouble for me!" said the cross woman.

"And for me!" said the angry fisherman.

"Send him away!" said the angry driver.

"But what about Tony?" asked the
Police Chief.

"If we send Mario away, Tony can-
not do his work."

Tony said, "Chief, I think I know a
better way."

Tony looked at the cross woman.

He said, "Mario ripped your sweater. My wife makes fine sweaters. She will make you another one."

"A green one?" said the woman.

"A green one," said Tony.

"With long sleeves?" said the woman.

"With long sleeves," said Tony.

"Fair enough," said the woman. She smiled.

Tony looked at the angry fisherman.

He said, "Mario made you lose your fish. I will show you a place with many fish."

"Big ones?" said the fisherman.

"Big ones," said Tony.

"Near here?" said the fisherman.

"Near here," said Tony.

"Fair enough," said the fisherman. He laughed.

Tony looked at the very angry driver.

He said, "Mario made you late for a meeting. What can we do to help?"

The driver said, "The meeting was about our school picnic. We need a bus to take the children out to the country. Can you tell us where to get one?"

Tony said, "I can do better than that.

"Mario and I will take the children in our wagon."

"This Saturday?" said the driver.

"This Saturday," said Tony.

"In the morning?" said the driver.

"In the morning," said Tony.

"Fair enough," said the driver. He shook hands.

The Police Chief smiled. "Mario may stay," he said.

"Lunch time, everyone!"

He looked around for his lunch box. It was gone.

"Where is my lunch?" he roared.

Mario had it. He was just eating the last sandwich.

Peanut butter and jam! It was good. He ate it all.

The Police Chief looked angry —
and very hungry.

Tony said, "My wife makes good
sandwiches, Chief. Mario and I will
bring you some more right away."

"Peanut butter and jam?" said the
Police Chief.

"Peanut butter and jam," said Tony.

"On brown bread?" said the Police Chief.

"On brown bread," said Tony.

"Fair enough," said the Police Chief. He looked happy again — but just as hungry.

Saturday morning came. Mario and Tony started out. Up and down the streets they went, picking up all the children. They went out into the country until they came to the river.

The children jumped off the wagon and opened their lunches. In every box, in every basket, and in every paper bag — there were sandwiches!

For the first time, Mario had all the
sandwiches he could eat.
Peanut butter . . .
Apple butter . . .
Jam . . .
Ham . . .
Chicken . . .
Egg . . .
and ice cream sandwiches!
Mario ate them all!

angry	peanut
around	place
country	police chief
driver	ripped
except	Saturday
fresh	sleeves
ham	shook
horn	sweater
jam	Tuesday
meeting	Thursday
Monday	trouble
oats	Wednesday